MW00910536

Princess Madison
and the Royal Darling Pageant

KAREN SCALF LINAMEN
ILLUSTRATED BY PHYLLIS HORNUNG

Revell
Grand Rapids, Michigan

Published by Fleming H. Revell
a division of Baker Publishing Group
P.O. Box 6287, Grand Rapids, MI 49516-6287

Printed in the United States of America

Library of Congress Cataloging-in-Publication Data
Linamen, Karen Scalf, 1960-
    Princess Madison and the Royal Darling Pageant / Karen Scalf Linamen ; illustrated by Phyllis Hornung.
        p. cm.
    Summary : In an attempt to prove to herself and her sister that she is a real princess, Madison looks for a frog to kiss, ends up sleeping on a small pea, and enters the Royal Darling Pageant in quest of a crown.
    ISBN 0-8007-1840-2 (cloth)
[1. Self-perception—Fiction. 2. Self-esteem—Fiction. 3. Princesses—Fiction. 4. Sisters—Fiction.]
I. Hornung, Phyllis, ill. II. Title.
PZ7.L6467Pri 2006
[E]—dc22
                                                                            2005016807

For Princess Kacie
and Princess Kaitlyn

Have you ever met a princess with dirt under her nails?

Or bangs that won't lie flat?

Or freckles on her nose?

How 'bout a princess with holes in her jeans?

Or marbles in her pockets?

Or a crown that won't behave?

Well, now you have, because Princess Madison is *exactly* that kind of princess.

You're probably thinking, *That's impossible! Princesses are supposed to be perfect. They're supposed to wear pink. They're supposed to drink tea with their pinkies in the air.*

That's what Evangeline thought too. Evangeline is Madison's big sister.

Evangeline is eleven and is precisely the kind of princess who wears pink, points her pinkie, and *thinks* she's perfect.

One sleepy winter afternoon outside the castle on Blue Moon Bay, snow clouds gathered quietly. Inside the castle Evangeline was *not* quiet. In fact, she was complaining about Madison to the cook in a loud and passionate voice.

"...*And* she hates pink. *And* she climbs trees. *And* her favorite thing to drink is Dr Pepper *from a can!*" huffed Evangeline.

"Girls are like snowflakes. No two are alike," said Cook.

"And she got a blister and wore the same Band-Aid for a *week*. How *embarrassing*," said Evangeline.

"Never judge a book by its cover," said Cook.

"I'll tell you what I think," said Evangeline.

"I'm sure you will," said Cook.

"I think she's not really a princess *at all*."

adison wanted to cry. She also wanted to sneak into her sister's room and break something, or maybe read Evangeline's diary and tell her friends what she *really* thought of them.

But part of her wondered if what Evangeline said was true.

What if Madison wasn't a real princess after all?

What if someone had given Madison to her parents for Christmas? What if she had been the kind of present you don't really want but you have to say thank you for anyway, kind of like when someone gives you new clothes, books without pictures, or even fruitcake?

Suddenly Madison knew *exactly* what she was going to do.

She wasn't going to cry.

Or break anything.

Or read Evangeline's diary *this time*.

Madison skipped all the way to Blue Moon Bay. Soon she would know if she was a real princess or not. All she had to do was catch a frog.

When she got there, the sky was gray. The water was gray too. The winter air felt damp and cold on Madison's face.

She searched the muddy banks with her eyes.

She parted soggy weeds with her hands.

She turned rocks with the toes of her shoes.

She sat down and listened. She could hear the throaty conversations of some frogs. Madison called "Brrrrrrbit" as loud as she could. She hoped she'd just said, "Come here, little frogs!" but she must have said, "Be quiet, every one of you!" because suddenly there was silence.

Now she heard only the water lapping at the shore. She heard a dog barking somewhere far away. A snowflake landed on her nose, then another, and another.

Behind the winter sky, the sun began to set. Madison headed home.

This time she didn't skip at all.

At the back door of the castle, Madison ran into Evangeline and her best friend, Sophie. Evangeline said to Sophie, "See? What did I tell you?"

Madison yelled, "I am too a princess! And I could have proved it by now if I'd found a frog. I'll show you I'm a real princess, you just wait and see!"

Evangeline began to laugh. "You were going to use Mom's jewelry box to catch a frog? And then you were going to *kiss it*?"

Madison stuck out her chin. "It worked for the princess in the fairy tale. When a *real* princess kisses a frog, he turns into a prince."

Evangeline said, "Sophie and I can prove if you're a real princess. Do you want our help?"

Madison crossed her arms. "Maybe. Maybe not."

Evangeline said, "Okay, we'll help. I'll tell you our plan in the morning." She grabbed Sophie's hand and pulled her toward the kitchen.

Madison made a beeline for Evangeline's room. She wasn't going to read her diary *today*, but she wanted to know if she was still stashing it behind the clothes hamper or if she'd found a new hiding place.

The next morning Madison blinked to find Evangeline and Sophie standing over her bed.

"How'd you sleep?" said Evangeline.

"Fine," said Madison.

"How fine?" said Sophie.

"Pretty fine," said Madison.

"That's too bad." Evangeline smirked.

Sophie held out a tiny green pea. "We put it under your mattress last night. You didn't even feel it."

"A real princess can feel a pea under a *hundred* mattresses," taunted Evangeline. "You couldn't feel it under *one*. Too bad, so sad." The big girls snickered and walked away.

Madison remembered a fairy tale about a princess and a pea. The princess *had* felt a pea under a hundred mattresses. That's how everyone knew she was a *real* princess. Now Madison *had* to know the truth.

Suddenly she laughed out loud. She gave herself a hug. Why hadn't she thought of this before?

Madison knew *exactly* what to do.

Several weeks went by. Encouraged by the sun, the clouds sent gentle rain instead of snow. Happy for the attention, the flowers and trees began to stretch and bud.

Springtime was coming to the royal kingdoms.

Which meant it was time for the Royal Darling Pageant.

Every spring little princesses from all the kingdoms gathered to take part in the pageant. The princess who won the pageant got a crown, a pony, and a ride in a hot air balloon.

Every year Madison's mother asked her if she wanted to be in the pageant. Every year Madison said no.

Until this year.

The morning of the pageant, Madison's mom, dad, and sister settled into their seats. Madison's father said, "Madison has worked very hard to get ready for this pageant." Her mother said, "I wonder why it's so important to her." Evangeline knew why, but she didn't say a word.

The lights dimmed. The curtain opened. Nine princesses stood in a line across the stage. Madison's heart was pounding so hard she wondered if it might leap away altogether. The music began.

The first princess stepped forward and curtsied. Holding the sides of her poofy skirt, she flashed a little smile between two perfect dimples.

The judges whispered. Then the one with the freckled ears said, "A lovely curtsy. Beautifully performed with a robust sense of rhythm and colorful timing. We give her a score of two tulips." Everyone clapped.

The second princess stepped forward. Her hair fell in golden ringlets halfway down her back. Madison thought she looked like Goldilocks. Madison wished Goldilocks would go visit some bears.

The judges said her curtsy had "extravagant balance" and gave Goldilocks a score of *three* tulips.

Suddenly it was Madison's turn. She tried to remember what to do.

Was she supposed to cross her knees and hold her head?

Or bend her smile and hold her dimples?

Shaking inside, Madison crossed one foot over the other. She held her skirt, bent her knees, nodded her head, and flashed a nervous smile. She did it!

The judges gave Madison one and a half tulips. They liked her "redundant continuity" and her "enigmatic execution."

As the curtains closed, Madison breathed a sigh of relief.

ext, each princess had to pour two cups of tea while chatting about the economy, which is exactly the kind of thing grown-up kings and queens have to do when they get important visitors from other countries.

Madison could never quite remember what an economy was, except that it could be good or bad and had something to do with money.

Using her most grown-up voice and spilling tea, she said, "So tell me, when was the last time you did something *so* bad that your parents took away your allowance for a week?"

The judge rolled his eyes toward the ceiling.

Madison wondered if he was mad, but he was just thinking.

He said, "It's been thirty-nine years. How long has it been for you?"

Madison said, "Last week. That's when my mother found my muddy clothes from the day I tried to catch the frog. It will probably happen again when she finds out that I'm the one who took her jewelry box as well."

Madison got *four* tulips.

Could Madison win the pageant? Could she win the crown that would prove to the world that she was a *very* real princess after all?

There was a short intermission. Madison's mom went to the lobby to buy a decaf skinny latte. Madison's dad went outside to make a call on his royal cell phone. Evangeline snuck backstage.

She found Madison in the dressing room kicking her feet nervously back and forth.

Evangeline said, "You're doing really good."

Madison said, "Thanks."

Evangeline said, "I've been thinking about that pea. You wouldn't believe how tiny it was. Now that I think about it, the pea in the fairy tale was a whole lot bigger."

One of the judges yelled, "Curtain goes up in three minutes!"

Evangeline said, "I'd better go."

Madison said, "Okay," although it didn't feel okay at all. Some days Madison wished she didn't even have a big sister, but today wasn't one of those days.

For the last part of the pageant, each princess got to reward a brave young man by making him a knight.

Here's how it works: the brave young man kneels in front of the royal person, who taps him gently on each shoulder with the flat edge of a sword and says, "I knight thee Sir Something or Other," giving the young man the new name he will use for the rest of his life, as well as a new suit of armor and a set of Ginsu steak knives.

Nine young men had been selected from throughout the kingdoms. Three of the men had fought dragons. Five had won battles against evil ogres. One had helped a senior citizen across a moat.

Goldilocks did fine. Dimples did fine. The other princesses did fine too.

Madison's knees began to shake. Someone put a sword in her hands. She closed her eyes. She heard a judge say, "Go ahead, dear."

As Madison lowered the sword, she said, "I . . . I knight thee Sir—"

Everyone gasped. Madison opened her eyes and dropped the sword. Her hands flew to her mouth, and she cried out, "Oh my goodness!"

The pageant ended without further mishap. Goldilocks won the crown, the pony, and the ride in the balloon.

The judge with the freckled ears spoke kindly to Madison's parents and told Madison he hoped her allowance would be reinstated before the end of the year.

Sir Ohmygoodness was treated for a small cut on his ear and given a baseball cap sporting the logo of the Royal Darling Pageant.

During the limo ride back to the castle on Blue Moon Bay, Madison was silent.

She was *very* upset.

When she got home, Madison went to her favorite hiding place to think. She thought about everything that had happened.

She hadn't turned a frog into a prince.

She hadn't felt the pea beneath her mattress.

She could barely curtsy, she couldn't pour tea without spilling, and she definitely couldn't knight anyone without drawing blood.

Evangeline was right. Madison wasn't a *real* princess after all.

A shadow fell across the henhouse doorway. The king ducked into the tiny shack and sat in the straw next to Madison. Madison wondered if there would be chicken poop on his pants when he stood up.

He said, "Evangeline told me everything." Madison's eyes filled with tears. Her father whispered, "But I'm here to tell you a secret. Would you like to know what it is?"

Madison blinked, and a tear spilled down her cheek.

Her father said, "Sweetheart, it's great for you to know how to curtsy or how to be polite or how to make someone a knight. Knowing how to act like a princess will serve you well all the days of your life.

"But here's the thing I need you to know. Princesses don't get to be princesses because they act a certain way; they get to be princesses because of who their father is. You're not a princess because of what you do or don't do. You're a princess because of your relationship to the king. Madison, you belong to me. That's what makes you a real princess." The king picked up Madison's crown from the straw. He brushed it off. He asked, "Would you like this back?"

Madison looked at her crown. She looked at her father.

Suddenly Madison smiled. She knew *exactly* what she wanted to do.

"The Father has loved us so much! He loved us so much that we are called children of God. And we really are his children." —1 John 3:1